GUESS
HOW MUCH
I LOVE YOU

To Liz with love,
A. J.

Text copyright © 1994 by Sam McBratney
Illustrations copyright © 1994 by Anita Jeram

Guess How Much I Love You™ is a registered trademark
of Walker Books Ltd., London.

First U.S. edition in this format 2008

The Library of Congress has cataloged the original hardcover edition as follows:

McBratney, Sam.
Guess how much I love you / by Sam McBratney ; illustrated by Anita Jeram. — 1st U.S. ed.
Summary: During a bedtime game, every time Little Nutbrown Hare demonstrates how much
he loves his father, Big Nutbrown Hare gently shows him that the love is returned even more.
ISBN 978-1-56402-473-2 (hardcover)
[1. Hares — Fiction. 2. Fathers and sons — Fiction. 3. Bedtime — Fiction. 4. Love — Fiction.]
I. Jeram, Anita, ill. II. Title.
PZ7.M47826Gu   1995
[E] — dc20   94-1599

ISBN 978-0-7636-4175-7 (large-format hardcover)

10 11 12 13 SCP 10 9 8 7 6

Printed in Humen, Dongguan, China

This book was typeset in Cochin.
The illustrations were done in ink and watercolor.

Candlewick Press
99 Dover Street
Somerville, Massachusetts 02144

visit us at www.candlewick.com

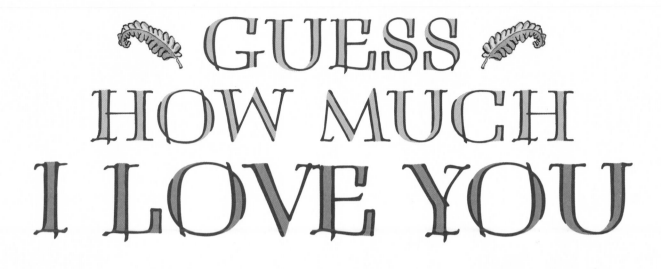

GUESS HOW MUCH I LOVE YOU

by
Sam McBratney

illustrated by
Anita Jeram

CANDLEWICK PRESS

Little Nutbrown Hare,
who was going to bed, held
on tight to Big Nutbrown Hare's
very long ears.

He wanted to be sure that Big
Nutbrown Hare was listening.
"Guess how much
I love you," he said.

"Oh, I don't think I could guess that,"
said Big Nutbrown Hare.

"This much," said Little
Nutbrown Hare, stretching out
his arms as wide as they could go.

Big Nutbrown Hare had even longer arms. "But I love *you* this much," he said.

Hmm, that is a lot, thought Little Nutbrown Hare.

"I love you as high as I can reach," said Little Nutbrown Hare.

"I love you
as high as
I can reach,"
said Big
Nutbrown
Hare.

That is quite
high, thought
Little Nutbrown
Hare. I wish
I had arms
like that.

Then Little
Nutbrown Hare
had a good idea.
He tumbled
upside down
and reached
up the tree
trunk with
his feet.

"I love you
all the way up
to my toes!"
he said.

"And *I* love you
all the way up
to your toes," said
Big Nutbrown Hare,
swinging him up
over his head.

"I love you
as high as
I can hop!"
laughed Little
Nutbrown Hare,

bouncing up

and down.

"But I love you as high as
I can hop," smiled Big
Nutbrown Hare – and he
hopped so high that his ears
touched the branches above.

That's good
hopping,
thought
Little
Nutbrown
Hare.
I wish I
could hop
like that.

"I love you all the way down the
lane as far as the river," cried
Little Nutbrown Hare.

"I love you across the river
and over the hills," said
Big Nutbrown Hare.

That's very far, thought
Little Nutbrown Hare.
He was almost too sleepy
to think any more.

Then he looked beyond the
thorn bushes, out into the big
dark night. Nothing could
be farther than the sky.

"I love you right up to
the moon," he said,
and closed his eyes.

"Oh, that's far," said
Big Nutbrown Hare.
"That is very,
very far."

Big Nutbrown Hare settled
Little Nutbrown Hare
into his bed of leaves.

He leaned over
and kissed him
good night.

Then he lay down close by
and whispered with a smile,
"I love you right up to the moon—

and back."